Sholem Aleichem: Five Short Stories

SHOLEM ALEICHEM

Translated by Helena Frank

Published by A. J. Cornell Publications
All rights reserved

ISBN-10: 149739662X
ISBN-13: 978-1497396623

CONTENTS

THE CLOCK

The clock struck thirteen!

Don't imagine I am joking, I am telling you in all seriousness what happened in Mazepevke, in our house, and I myself was there at the time.

We had a clock, a large clock, fastened to the wall, an old, old clock inherited from my grandfather, which had been left him by my great-grandfather, and so forth. Too bad, that a clock should not be alive and able to tell us something beside the time of day! What stories we might have heard as we sat with it in the room! Our clock was famous throughout the town as the best clock going—Reb Simcheh's clock"—and people used to come and set their watches by it, because it kept more accurate time than any other. You may believe me that even Reb Lebish, the sage, a philosopher, who understood the time of sunset from the sun itself, and knew the calendar by rote, he said himself—I heard him—that our clock was—well, as compared with his watch, it wasn't worth a pinch of snuff, but as there *were* such things as clocks, our clock *was* a clock. And if Reb Lebish himself said so, you may depend upon it he was right, because every Wednesday, between Afternoon and Evening Prayer, Reb Lebish climbed busily onto the roof of the women's Shool, or onto the top of the hill beside the old house-of-study, and looked out for the minute when the sun should set, in one hand his watch, and in the other the calendar. And when the sun dropt out of sight on the further side of Mazepevke, Reb Lebish said to himself, "Got him!" and at once came away to compare his watch with the clocks. When he came in to us, he never gave us a "good evening," only glanced up at the clock on the wall, then at his watch, then at the almanac, and was gone!

But it happencd one day that when Reb Lebish came in to compare our clock with the almanac, he gave a shout:

"Sim-cheh! Make haste! Where are you?"

My father came running in terror.

"Ha, what has happened, Reb Lebish?"

"Wretch, you dare to ask?" and Reb Lebish held his watch under my father's nose, pointed at our clock, and shouted again, like a man with a trodden toe:

"Sim-cheh! Why don't you speak? It is a minute and a half ahead of the time! Throw it away!"

My father was vexed. What did Reb Lebish mean by telling him to throw away his clock?

"Who is to prove," said he, "that my clock is a minute and a half fast? Perhaps it is the other way about, and your watch is a minute and a half slow? Who is to tell?"

Reb Lebish stared at him as though he had said that it was possible to have three days of New Moon, or that the Seventeenth of Tammuz might possibly fall on the Eve of Passover, or made some other such wild remark, enough,

2

if one really took it in, to give one an apoplectic fit. Reb Lebish said never a word, he gave a deep sigh, turned away without wishing us "good evening," slammed the door, and was gone. But no one minded much, because the whole town knew Reb Lebish for a person who was never satisfied with anything: he would tell you of the best cantor that he was a dummy, a log; of the cleverest man, that he was a lumbering animal; of the most appropriate match, that it was as crooked as an oven rake; and of the most apt simile, that it was as applicable as a pea to the wall. Such a man was Reb Lebish.

But let me return to our clock. I tell you, that *was* a clock! You could hear it strike three rooms away: Bom! bom! bom! Half the town went by it, to recite the Midnight Prayers, to get up early for Seliches during the week before New Year and on the ten Solemn Days, to bake the Sabbath loaves on Fridays, to bless the candles on Friday evening. They lighted the fire by it on Saturday evening, they salted the meat, and so all the other things pertaining to Judaism. In fact, our clock was the town clock. The poor thing served us faithfully, and never tried stopping even for a time, never once in its life had it to be set to rights by a clockmaker. My father kept it in order himself, he had an inborn talent for clock work. Every year on the Eve of Passover, he deliberately took it down from the wall, dusted the wheels with a feather brush, removed from its inward part a collection of spider webs, desiccated flies, which the spiders had lured in there to their destruction, and heaps of black cockroaches, which had gone in of themselves, and found a terrible end. Having cleaned and polished it, he hung it up again on the wall and shone, that is, they both shone: the clock shone because it was cleaned and polished, and my father shone because the clock shone.

And it came to pass one day that something happened.

It was on a fine, bright, cloudless day; we were all sitting at table, eating breakfast, and the clock struck. Now I always loved to hear the clock strike and count the strokes out loud:

"One—two—three—seven—eleven—twelve—thirteen! Oi! *Thirteen?*"

"Thirteen?" exclaimed my father, and laughed, "You're a fine arithmetician (no evil eye!). Whenever did you hear a clock strike thirteen?"

"But I tell you, it *struck* thirteen!"

"I shall give you thirteen slaps," cried my father, angrily, "and then you won't repeat this nonsense again. Goi, a clock *cannot* strike thirteen!"

"Do you know what, Simcheh," put in my mother, "I am afraid the child is right, I fancy I counted thirteen, too."

"There's another witness!" said my father, but it appeared that he had begun to feel a little doubtful himself, for after the meal he went up to the clock, got upon a chair, gave a turn to a little wheel inside the clock, and it began to strike. We all counted the strokes, nodding our head at each one the while: one—two—three—seven—nine—twelve—thirteen.

"Thirteen!" exclaimed my father, looking at us in amazement. He gave the wheel another turn, and again the clock struck thirteen. My father got down off the chair with a sigh. He was as white as the wall, and remained standing in the middle of the room, stared at the ceiling, chewed his beard, and muttered to himself:

"Plague take thirteen! What can it mean? What does it portend? If it were out of order, it would have stopped. Then, what can it be? The inference can only be that some spring has gone wrong."

"Why worry whether it's a spring or not?" said my mother. "You'd better take down the clock and put it to rights, as you've a turn that way."

"Hush, perhaps you're right," answered my father, took down the clock and busied himself with it. He perspired, spent a whole day over it, and hung it up again in its place.

Thank God, the clock was going as it should, and when, near midnight, we all stood round it and counted *twelve*, my father was overjoyed.

"Ha? It didn't strike thirteen then, did it? When I say it is a spring, I know what I'm about."

"I always said you were a wonder," my mother told him. "But there is one thing I don't understand: why does it wheeze so? I don't think it used to wheeze like that."

"It's your fancy," said my father, and listened to the noise it made before striking, like an old man preparing to cough: chil-chil-chil-chil-trrrr…and only then: bom!—bom!—bom!—and even the "bom" was not the same as formerly, for the former "bom" had been a cheerful one, and now there had crept into it a melancholy note, as into the voice of an old worn-out cantor at the close of the service for the Day of Atonement, and the hoarseness increased, and the strike became lower and duller, and my father, worried and anxious. It was plain that the affair preyed upon his mind, that he suffered in secret, that it was undermining his health, and yet he could do nothing. We felt that any moment the clock might stop altogether.

The imp started playing all kinds of nasty tricks and idle pranks, shook itself sideways, and stumbled like an old man who drags his feet after him. One could see that the clock was about to stop forever! It was a good thing my father understood in time that the clock was about to yield up its soul, and that the fault lay with the balance weights: the weight was too light. And he puts on a jostle, which has the weight of about four pounds. The clock goes on like a song, and my father becomes as cheerful as a newborn man.

But this was not to be for long: the clock began to lose again, the imp was back at his tiresome performances: he moved slowly on one side, quickly on the other, with a hoarse noise, like a sick old man, so that it went to the heart. A pity to see how the clock agonized, and my father, as he watched it, seemed like a flickering, bickering flame of a candle, and nearly went out for grief.

Like a good doctor, who is ready to sacrifice himself for the patient's sake, who puts forth all his energy, tries every remedy under the sun to save his patient, even so my father applied himself to save the old clock, if only it should be possible.

"The weight is too light," repeated my father, and hung something heavier onto it every time, first a frying pan, then a copper jug, afterwards a flat-iron, a bag of sand, a couple of tiles—and the clock revived every time and went on, with difficulty and distress, but still it went— till one night there was a misfortune.

It was on a Friday evening in winter. We had just eaten our Sabbath supper, the delicious peppered fish with horseradish, the hot soup with macaroni, the stewed plums, and said grace as was meet. The Sabbath candles flickered, the maid was just handing round fresh, hot, well-dried Polish nuts from off the top of the stove, when in came Aunt Yente, a dark-favored little woman without teeth, whose husband had deserted her, to become a follower of the Rebbe, quite a number of years ago.

"Good Sabbath!" said Aunt Yente, "I knew you had some fresh Polish nuts. The pity is that I've nothing to crack them with, may my husband live no more years than I have teeth in my mouth! What did you think, Malkeh, of the fish today? What a struggle there was over them at the market! I asked him about his fish—Manasseh, the lazy—when up comes Soreh Peril, the rich: Make haste, give it me, hand me over that little pike!—Why in such a hurry? say I. God be with you, the river is not on fire, and Manasseh is not going to take the fish back there, either. Take my word for it, with these rich people money is cheap, and sense is dear. Turns round on me and says: Paupers, she says, have no business here—a poor man, she says, shouldn't hanker after good things. What do you think of such a shrew? How long did she stand by her mother in the market selling ribbons? She behaves just like Pessil Peise Avròhom's over her daughter, the one she married to a great man in Schtrischtch, who took her just as she was, without any dowry or anything—Jewish luck! They say she has a bad time of it—no evil eye to her days—can't get on with his children. Well, who would be a stepmother? Let them beware! Take Chavvehle! What is there to find fault with in her? And you should see the life her stepchildren lead her! One hears shouting day and night, cursing, squabbling, and fighting."

The candles began to die down, the shadow climbed the wall, scrambled higher and higher, the nuts crackled in our hands, there was talking and telling stories and tales, just for the pleasure of it, one without any reference to the other, but Aunt Yente talked more than anyone.

"Hush!" Cried out Aunt Yente, "listen, because not long ago a still better thing happened. Not far from Yampele, about three versts [two miles] away, some robbers fell upon a Jewish tavern, killed a whole houseful of people, down to a baby in a cradle. The only person left alive was a servant-girl, who was sleeping on the kitchen stove. She heard people screeching, and jumped down, this servant-girl, off the stove, peeped through a chink in the door, and saw, this servant-girl I'm telling you of, saw the master of the house and the mistress lying on the floor, murdered, in a pool of blood, and she went back, this girl, and sprang through a window, and ran into the town screaming: Jews, to the rescue, help, help, help!"

Suddenly, just as Aunt Yente was shouting, "Help, help, help!" we heard *trrraach!—tarrrach!—bom—dzin—dzin—dzin, bomm!!* We were so deep in the story, we only thought at first that robbers had descended upon our house, and were firing guns, and we could not move for terror. For one minute we looked at one another, and then with one accord we began to call out, "Help! help! help!" and my mother was so carried away that she clasped me in her arms and cried: "My child, my life for yours, woe is me!" "Ha? What? What is the matter with him? What has happened?" exclaimed my father.

"Nothing! nothing! hush! hush!" cried Aunt Yente, gesticulating wildly, and the maid came running in from the kitchen, more dead than alive.

"Who screamed? What is it? Is there a fire? What is on fire? Where?"

"Fire? fire? Where is the fire?" we all shrieked. "Help! help! Gewalt, Jews, to the rescue, fire, fire!"

"Which fire? what fire? where fire?! Fire take *you*, you foolish girl, and make cinders of you!" scolded Aunt Yente at the maid. "Now she must come, as though we weren't enough before! Fire, indeed, says she! Into the earth with you, to all black years! Did you ever hear of such a thing? What are you all yelling for? Do you know what it was that frightened you? The best joke in the world, and there's nobody to laugh with! God be with you, it was the clock falling onto the floor—now you know! You hung every sort of thing onto it, and now it is fallen, weighing at least three pud. And no wonder! A man wouldn't have fared better. Did you ever?!"

It was only then we came to our senses, rose one by one from the table, went to the clock, and saw it lying on its poor face, killed, broken, shattered, and smashed for evermore!

"There is an end to the clock!" said my father, white as the wall. He hung his head, wrung his fingers, and the tears came into his eyes. I looked at my father and wanted to cry, too.

"There now, see, what is the use of fretting to death?" said my mother. "No doubt it was so decreed and written down in Heaven that today, at that particular minute, our clock was to find its end, just (I beg to distinguish!) like a human being, may God not punish me for saying so! May it be an Atonement for not remembering the Sabbath, for me, for thee, for our children, for all near and dear to us, and for all Israel. Amen, Selah!"

FISHEL THE TEACHER

Twice a year, as sure as the clock, on the first day of Nisan and the first of Ellul—for Passover and Tabernacles—Fishel the teacher traveled from Balta to Chaschtschevate, home to his wife and children. It was decreed that nearly all his life long he should be the guest of his own family, a very welcome guest, but a passing one. He came with the festival, and no sooner was it over, than back with him to Balta, back to the schooling, the ruler, the Gemoreh, the dull, thick wits, to the being knocked about from pillar to post, to the wandering among strangers, and the longing for home.

On the other hand, when Fishel *does* come home, he is an emperor! His wife Bathsheba comes out to meet him, pulls at her head-kerchief, blushes red as fire, questions as though in asides, without as yet looking him in the face, "How are you?" and he replies, "How are *you?*" and Froike his son, a boy of thirteen or so, greets him, and the father asks, "Well, Efroim, and how far on are you in the Gemoreh?" and his little daughter Resele, not at all a bad-

10

looking little girl, with a plaited pigtail, hugs and kisses him.

"Tate, what sort of present have you brought me?"

"Printed calico for a frock, and a silk kerchief for mother. There—give mother the kerchief!"

And Fishel takes a silk (suppose a half-silk!) kerchief out of his Tallis-bag, and Bath-sheba grows redder still, and pulls her head-cloth over her eyes, takes up a bit of household work, busies herself all over the place, and ends by doing nothing.

"Bring the Gemoreh, Efroim, and let me hear what you can do!"

And Froike recites his lesson like the bright boy he is, and Fishel listens and corrects, and his heart expands and overflows with delight, his soul rejoices—a bright boy, Froike, a treasure!

"If you want to go to the bath, there is a shirt ready for you!"

Thus Bath-sheba as she passes him, still not venturing to look him in the face, and Fishel has a sensation of unspeakable comfort, he feels like a man escaped from prison and back in a lightsome world, among those who are near and dear to him. And he sees in fancy a very, very hot bathhouse, and himself lying on the highest bench with other Jews, and he perspires and swishes himself with the birch twigs, and can never have enough.

Home from the bath, fresh and lively as a fish, like one newborn, he rehearses the portion of the Law for the festival, puts on the Sabbath cloak and the new girdle, steals a glance at Bath-sheba in her new dress and silk kerchief—still a pretty woman, and so pious and good!— and goes with France to the Shool. The air is full of

Sholom Aleichem's, "Welcome, Reb Fishel the teacher, and what are you about?"—"A teacher teaches!"—"What is the news?"—"What should it be? The world is the world!"—"What is going on in Balta?"—"Balta is Balta."

The same formula is repeated every time, every half-year, and Nissel the reader begins to recite the evening prayers, and sends forth his voice, the further the louder, and when he comes to "And Moses declared the set feasts of the Lord unto the children of Israel," it reaches nearly to Heaven. And Froike stands at his father's side, and recites the prayers melodiously, and once more Fishel's heart expands and flows over with joy—a good child, Froike, a good, pious child!

"A happy holiday, a happy holiday!"

"A happy holiday, a happy year!"

At home they find the Passover table spread: the four cups, the bitter herbs, the almond and apple paste, and all the rest of it. The reclining-seats (two small benches with big cushions) stand ready, and Fishel becomes a king. Fishel, robed in white, sits on the throne of his dominion, Bath-sheba, the queen, sits beside him in her new silk kerchief; Efroim, the prince, in a new cap, and the princess Resele with her plait, sit opposite them. Look on with respect! His majesty Fishel is seated on his throne, and has assumed the sway of his kingdom.

The Chaschtschevate scamps, who love to make game of the whole world, not to mention a teacher, maintain that one Passover Eve our Fishel sent his Bath-sheba the following Russian telegram: "Rebyàtà sobral dyèngi vezù prigatovi npiyèdu tzàrstvovàtz," which means: "Have entered my pupils for the next term, am bringing money, prepare the dumplings, I come to reign." The mischief-makers declare that this telegram was seized at Balta station, that Bath-sheba was sought and not found, and that Fisher was sent home with the tape. Dreadful! But I can assure you, there isn't a word of truth in the story, because Fishel never sent a telegram in his life, nobody was ever seen looking for Bath-sheba, and Fishel was never taken anywhere by the étape. That is, he *was* once taken somewhere by the étape, but not on account of a telegram, only on account of a simple passport! And not from Balta, but from Yehupetz, and not at Passover, but in summertime. He wished, you see, to go to Yehupetz in search of a post as teacher, and forgot his passport. He thought it was in Balta, and he got into a nice mess, and forbade his children and children's children ever to go in search of pupils in Yehupetz.

Since then he teaches in Balta, and comes home for Passover, winds up his work a fortnight earlier, and sometimes manages to hasten back in time for the Great Sabbath. Hasten, did I say? That means when the road is a road, when you can hire a conveyance, and when the Bug can either be crossed on the ice or in the ferryboat. But when, for instance, the snow has begun to melt, and the mud is deep, when there is no conveyance to be had, when the Bug has begun to split the ice, and the ferry-boat has not started running, when a skiff means peril of death, and the festival is upon you—what then? It is just "nit güt."

Fishel the teacher knows the taste of "nit güt." He has had many adventures and mishaps since he became a teacher, and took to faring from Chaschtschevate to Balta and from Balta to Chaschtschevate. He has tried going more than halfway on foot, and helped to push the conveyance besides. He has lain in the mud with a priest, the priest on top, and he below. He has fled before a pack of wolves who were pursuing the vehicle, and afterwards they turned out to be dogs, and not wolves at all. But anything like the trouble on this Passover Eve had never befallen him before.

The trouble came from the Bug, that is, from the bugs breaking through the ice, and just having its fling when Fishel reached it in a hurry to get home, and really in a hurry, because it was already Friday and Passover Eve, that is, Passover eve fell on a Sabbath that year.

Fishel reached the Bug in a Gentile conveyance Thursday evening. According to his own reckoning, he should have got there Tuesday morning, because he left Balta Sunday after market, the spirit having moved him to go into the marketplace to spy after a chance conveyance. How much better it would have been to drive with Yainkel-Shegetz, a Balta carrier, even at the cart-tail, with his legs dangling, and shaken to bits. He would have been home long ago by now, and have forgotten the discomforts of the journey. But he had wanted a cheaper transit, and it is an old saying that cheap things cost dear. Yoneh, the tippler, who procures vehicles in Balta, had said to him: "Take my advice, give two rubles, and you will ride in Yainkel's wagon like a lord, even if you do have to sit behind the wagon. Consider, you're playing with fire, the festival approaches." But as ill-luck would have it, there came along a familiar Gentile from Chaschtschevate.

"Eh, Rabbi, you're not wanting a lift to Chaschtschevate?"

"How much would the fare be?"

He thought to ask how much, and he never thought to

14

ask if it would take him home by Passover, because in a week he could have covered the distance walking behind the cart.

But as Fisher drove out of the town, he soon began to repent of his choice, even though the wagon was large, and he sitting in it in solitary grandeur, like any count. He saw that with a horse that dragged itself along in that way, there would be no getting far, for they drove a whole day without getting anywhere in particular, and however much he worried the peasant to know if it were a long way yet, the only reply he got was, "Who can tell?" In the evening, with a rumble and a shout and a crack of the whip, there came up with them Yainkel-Shegetz and his four fiery horses jingling with bells, and the large coach packed with passengers before and behind. Yainkel, catching sight of the teacher in the peasant's cart, gave another loud crack with his whip, ridiculed the peasant, his passenger, and his horse, as only Yainkel-Shegetz knows how, and when a little way off, he turned and pointed at one of the peasant's wheels.

"Hallo, man, look out! There's a wheel turning!"

The peasant stopped the horse, and he and the teacher clambered down together, and examined the wheels. They crawled underneath the cart, and found nothing wrong, nothing at all.

When the peasant understood that Yainkel had made a fool of him, he scratched the back of his neck below his collar, and began to abuse Yainkel and all Jews with curses such as Fishel had never heard before. His voice and his anger rose together:

"May you never know good! May you have a bad year! May you not see the end of it! Bad luck to you, you and your horses and your wife and your daughter and your aunts and your uncles and your parents-in-law and—and all your cursed Jews!"

It was a long time before the peasant took his seat again, nor did he cease to fume against Yainkel the driver and all Jews, until, with God's help, they reached a village wherein to spend the night.

Next morning Fishel rose with the dawn, recited his prayers, a portion of the Law, and a few Psalms, breakfasted on a roll, and was ready to set forward. Unfortunately, Chfedor (this was the name of his driver) was *not* ready. Chfedor had sat up late with a crony and got drunk, and he slept through a whole day and a bit of the night, and then only started on his way.

"Well," Fishel reproved him as they sat in the cart, "well, Chfedor, a nice way to behave, upon my word! Do you suppose I engaged you for a merrymaking? What have you to say for yourself, I should like to know, eh?"

And Fishel addressed other reproachful words to him, and never ceased casting the other's laziness between his teeth, partly in Polish, partly in Hebrew, and helping himself out with his hands. Chfedor understood quite well what Fishel meant, but he answered him not a word, not a syllable even. No doubt he felt that Fishel was in the right, and he was silent as a cat, till, on the fourth day, they met Yainkel-Shegetz, driving back from Chaschtschevate with a rumble and a crack of his whip, who called out to them, "You may as well turn back to Balta, the Bug has burst the ice."

Fishel's heart was like to burst, too, but Chfedor, who thought that Yainkel was trying to fool him a second time, started repeating his whole list of curses, called down all bad dreams on Yainkel's hands and feet, and never shut his mouth till they came to the Bug on Thursday evening. They drove straight to Prokop Baranyùk, the ferryman, to inquire when the ferryboat would begin to run, and the two Gentiles, Chfedor and Prokop, took to sipping brandy, while Fishel proceeded to recite the Afternoon Prayer.

The sun was about to set, and poured a rosy light onto the high hills that stood on either side of the river, and were snow-covered in parts and already green in others, and intersected by rivulets that wound their way with murmuring noise down into the river, where the water foamed with the broken ice and the increasing thaw. The whole of Chaschtschevate lay before him as on a plate, while the top of the monastery sparkled like a light in the setting sun. Standing to recite the Eighteen Benedictions, with his face towards Chaschtschevate, Fishel turned his eyes away and drove out the idle thoughts and images that had crept into his head: Bathsheba with the new silk kerchief, Froike with the Gemoreh, Resele with her plait, the hot bath and the highest bench, and freshly baked Matzes, together with nice peppered fish and horseradish that goes up your nose, Passover borsht with more Matzes, a heavenly mixture, and all the other good things that desire is capable of conjuring up—and however often he drove these fancies away, they returned and crept back into his brain like summer flies, and disturbed him at his prayers.

When Fishel had repeated the Eighteen Benedictions and Olenu, he betook him to Prokop, and entered into conversation with him about the ferryboat and the festival eve, giving him to understand, partly in Polish and partly in Hebrew and partly with his hands, what Passover meant to the Jews, and Passover Eve falling on a Sabbath, and that if, which Heaven forbid, he had not crossed the Bug by that time tomorrow, he was a lost man, for, beside the fact that they were on the lookout for him at home—his wife and children (Fisher gave a sigh that rent the heart)—he would not be able to eat or drink for a week, and Fishel turned away, so that the tears in his eyes should not be seen.

Prokop Baranyùk quite appreciated Fishel's position, and replied that he knew tomorrow was a Jewish festival, and even how it was called; he even knew that the Jews celebrated it by drinking wine and strong brandy; he even knew that there was yet another festival at which the Jews drank brandy, and a third when all Jews were obliged to get drunk, but he had forgotten its name—

"Well and good," Fishel interrupted him in a lamentable voice, "but what is to happen? How if I don't get there?"

To this Prokop made no reply. He merely pointed with his hand to the river, as much as to say, "See for yourself!"

And Fishel lifted up his eyes to the river, and saw that which he had never seen before, and heard that which he had never heard in his life. Because you may say that Fisher had never yet taken in anything "out of doors," he had only perceived it accidentally, by the way, as he hurried from Cheder to the house-of-study, and from the house-of-study to Cheder. The beautiful blue Bug between the two lines of imposing hills, the murmur of the winding rivulets as they poured down the hillsides, the roar of the ever-deepening spring-flow, the light of the setting sun, the glittering cupola of the convent, the wholesome smell of Passover-Eve-tide out of doors, and, above all, the being so close to home and not able to get there—all these things lent wings, as it were, to Fisher's spirit, and he was borne into a new world, the world of imagination, and crossing the bug seemed the merest trifle, if only the Almighty were willing to perform a fraction of a miracle on his behalf.

Such and like thoughts floated in and out of Fishel's head, and lifted him into the air, and so far across the river, he never realized that it was night, and the stars came out, and a cool wind blew in under his cloak to his little prayer-scarf, and Fishel was busy with things that he had never so much as dreamt of: earthly things and Heavenly things, the great size of the beautiful world, the Almighty as Creator of the earth, and so on.

Fishel spent a bad night in Prokop's house—such a night as he hoped never to spend again. The next morning broke with a smile from the bright and cheerful sun. It was a singularly fine day, and so sweetly warm that all the snow left melted into kasha, and the kasha, into water, and this water poured into the Bug from all sides; and the Bug became clearer, light blue, full and smooth, and the large bits of ice that looked like dreadful wild beasts, like white elephants hurrying and tearing along as if they were afraid of being late, grew rarer.

Fishel the teacher recited the Morning Prayer, breakfasted on the last piece of leavened bread left in his prayer-scarf bag, and went out to the river to see about the ferry. Imagine his feelings when he heard that the ferryboat would not begin running before Sunday afternoon! He clapped both hands to his head, gesticulated with every limb, and fell to abusing Prokop. Why had he given him hopes of the ferryboat's crossing next day? Whereupon Prokop answered quite coolly that he had said nothing about crossing with the ferry, he was talking of taking him across in a small boat! And that he could still do, if Fishel wished, in a sailboat, in a rowboat, in a raft, and the fare was not less than one ruble.

"A raft, a rowboat, anything you like, only don't let me spend the festival away from home!"

Thus Fishel, and he was prepared to give him two rubles then and there, to give his life for the holy festival, and he began to drive Prokop into getting out the raft at once, and taking him across in the direction of Chaschtschevate, where Bath-sheba, Froike, and resale are already looking out for him. It may he they are standing on the opposite hills, that they see him, and make signs to him, waving their hands, that they call to him, only one can neither see them nor hear their voices, because the river is wide, dreadfully wide, wider than ever!

The sun was already half-way up the deep, blue sky, when Prokop told Fishel to get into the little trough of a boat, and when Fishel heard him, he lost all power in his feet and hands, and was at a loss what to do, for never in his life had he been in a rowboat, never in his life had he been in any small boat. And it seemed to him the thing had only to dip a little to one side, and all would be over.

"Jump in, and off we'll go!" said Prokop once more, and with a turn of his oar he brought the boat still closer in, and took Fishel's bundle out of his hands.

Fishel the teacher drew his coat-skirts neatly together, and began to perform circles without moving from the spot, hesitating whether to jump or not. On the one hand were Passover Eve, Bath-sheba, France, Resele, the bath, the home service, himself as king; on the other, peril of death, the Destroying Angel, suicide—because one dip and—good-by, Fishel, peace be upon him!

And Fishel remained circling there with his folded skirts, till Prokop lost patience and said, another minute, and he should set out and be off to Chaschtschevate without him. At the beloved word "Chaschtschevate," Fishel called his dear ones to mind, summoned the whole of his courage, and fell into the boat. I say "fell in," because the instant his foot touched the bottom of the boat, it slipped, and Fishel, thinking he was falling, drew back, and this drawing back sent him headlong forward into the boat-bottom, where he lay stretched out for some minutes before recovering his wits, and for a long time after his face was livid, and his hands shook, while his heart beat like a clock, tik-tik-tak, tik-tik-tak!

Prokop meantime sat in the prow as though he were at home. He spit into his hands, gave a stroke with the oar to the left, a stroke to the right, and the boat glided over the shining water, and Fisher's head spun round as he sat. As he sat? No, he hung floating, suspended in the air! One false movement, and that which held him would give way; one lean to the side, and he would be in the water and done with! At this thought, the words came into his mind, "And they sank like lead in the mighty waters," and his hair stood on end at the idea of such a death. How? Not even to be buried with the dead of Israel? And he bethought himself to make a vow to—to do what? To give money in charity? He had none to give—he was a very, very poor man! So he vowed that if God would bring him

21

home in safety, he would sit up whole nights and study, go through the whole of the Talmud in one year, God willing, with God's help.

Fishel would dearly have liked to know if it were much further to the other side, and found himself seated, as though on purpose, with his face to Prokop and his back to Chaschtschevate. And he dared not open his mouth to ask. It seemed to him that his very voice would cause the boat to rock, and one rock—good-by, Fishel! But Prokop opened his mouth of his own accord, and began to speak. He said there was nothing worse when you were on the water than a thaw. It made it impossible, he said, to row straight ahead; one had to adapt one's course to the ice, to row round and round and backwards.

"There's a bit of ice making straight for us now."

Thus Prokop, and he pulled back and let pass a regular ice-floe, which swam by with a singular rocking motion and a sound that Fisher had never seen or heard before. And then he began to understand what a wild adventure this journey was, and he would have given goodness knows what to be safe on shore, even on the one they had left.

"O, you see that?" asked Prokop, and pointed upstream.

Fishel raised his eyes slowly, was afraid of moving much, and looked and looked, and saw nothing but water, water, and water.

"There's a big one coming down on us now, we must make a dash for it, for it's too late to row back."

So said Prokop, and rowed away with both hands, and the boat glided and slid like a fish through the water, and Fishel felt cold in every limb. He would have liked to question, but was afraid of interfering. However, again Prokop spoke of himself.

"If we don't win by a minute, it will be the worse for us."

Fishel can now no longer contain himself, and asks: "How do you mean, the worse?" "We shall be done for," says Prokop. "Done for?" "Done for."

"How do you mean, done for?" persists Fishel. "I mean, it will grind us." "Grind us?"

"Grind us."

Fisher does not understand what "grind us, grind us" may signify, but it has a sound of finality, of the next world, about it, and Fishel is bathed in a cold sweat, and again the words come into his head, "And they sank like lead in the mighty waters."

And Prokop, as though to quiet our Fishel's mind, tells him a comforting story of how, years ago at this time, the Bug broke through the ice, and the ferryboat could not be used, and there came to him another person to be rowed across, an excise official from Uman, quite a person of distinction, and offered a large sum; and they had the bad luck to meet two huge pieces of ice, and he rowed to the right, in between the floes, intending to slip through upwards, and he made an involuntary side motion with the boat, and they went flop into the water! Fortunately, he, Prokop, could swim, but the official came to grief, and the fare-money, too.

"It was good-by to my fare!" ended Prokop, with a sigh, and Fishel shuddered, and his tongue dried up, so that he could neither speak nor utter the slightest sound.

In the very middle of the river, just as they were rowing along quite smoothly, Prokop suddenly stopped, and looked—and looked—up the stream; then he laid down the oars, drew a bottle out of his pocket, tilted it into his mouth, sipped out of it two or three times, put it back, and explained to Fisher that he had always to take a few sips of the "bitter drop," otherwise he felt bad when on the water. And he wiped his mouth, took the oars in hand again, and said, having crossed himself three times:

"Now for a race!"

A race? With whom? With what? Fishel did not understand, and was afraid to ask; but again he felt the brush of the Death Angel's wing, for Prokop had gone down onto his knees, and was rowing with might and main. Moreover, he said to Fishel, and pointed to the bottom of the boat:

"Rebbe, lie down!"

Fishel understood that he was to lie down, and did not need to be told twice. For now he had seen a whole host of floes coming down upon them, a world of ice, and he shut his eyes, flung himself face downwards in the boat, and lay trembling like a lamb, and recited in a low voice, "Hear, O Israel!" and the Confession, thought on the graves of Israel, and fancied that now, now he lies in the abyss of the waters, now, now comes a fish and swallows him, like Jonah the prophet when he fled to Tarshish, and he remembers Jonah's prayer, and sings softly and with tears:

"Affofùni màyyim ad nòfesh—the waters have reached unto my soul; tehòm yesovevèni—the deep hath covered me!"

Fishel the teacher sang and wept and thought pitifully of his widowed wife and his orphaned children, and Prokop rowed for all he was worth, and sang *his* little song:

"O thou maiden with the black lashes!"

And Prokop felt the same on the water as on dry land, and Fishel's "Affofùni" and Prokop's "O maiden" blended into one, and a strange song sounded over the Bug, a kind of duet, which had never been heard there before.

"The black year knows why he is so afraid of death, that Jew," so wondered Prokop Baranyùk, "a poor tattered little Jew like him, a creature I would not give this old boat for, and so afraid of death!"

The shore reached, Prokop gave Fishel a shove in the side with his boot, and Fishel started. The Gentile burst out laughing, but Fisher did not hear, Fisher went on reciting the Confession, saying Kaddish for his own soul, and mentally contemplating the graves of Israel!

"Get up, you silly Rebbe! We're there—in Chaschtschevate!"

Slowly, slowly, Fishel raised his head, and gazed around him with red and swollen eyes.

"Chasch-tsche-va-te???"

"Chaschtschevate! Give me the ruble, Rebbe!"

Fishel crawls out of the boat, and, finding himself really at home, does not know what to do for joy. Shall he run into the town? Shall he go dancing? Shall he first thank and praise God who has brought him safe out of such great peril? He pays the Gentile his fare, takes up his bundle under his arm and is about to run home, the quicker the better, but he pauses a moment first, and turns to Prokop the ferryman:

"Listen, Prokop, dear heart, tomorrow, please God, you'll come and drink a glass of brandy, and taste festival fish at Fishel the teacher's, for Heaven's sake!"

"Shall I say no? Am I such a fool?" replied Prokop,

licking his lips in anticipation at the thought of the Passover brandy he would sip, and the festival fish he would delectate himself with on the morrow.

And Prokop gets back into his boat, and pulls quietly home again, singing a little song, and pitying the poor Jew who was so afraid of death. "The Jewish faith is the same as the Mohammedan!" and it seems to him a very foolish one. And Fishel is thinking almost the same thing, and pities the Gentile on account of *his* religion. "What knows he, yon poor Gentile, of such holy promises as were made to us Jews, the beloved people!"

And Fishel the teacher hastens uphill, through the Chaschtschevate mud. He perspires with the exertion, and yet he does not feel the ground beneath his feet. He flies, he floats, he is going home, home to his dear ones, who are on the watch for him as for Messiah, who look for him to return in health, to seat himself upon his kingly throne and reign.

Look, Jews, and turn respectfully aside! Fishel the teacher has come home to Chaschtschevate, and seated himself upon the throne of his kingdom!

AN EASY FAST

That which Doctor Tanner failed to accomplish, was effectually carried out by Chayyim Chaikin, a simple Jew in a small town in Poland.

Doctor Tanner wished to show that a man can fast forty days, and he only managed to get through twenty-eight, no more, and that with people pouring spoonfuls of water into his mouth, and giving him morsels of ice to swallow, and holding his pulse—a whole business! Chayyim Chaikin has proved that one can fast more than forty days; not, as a rule, two together, one after the other, but forty days, if not more, in the course of a year.

To fast is all he asks!

Who said drops of water? Who said ice? Not for him! To fast means no food and no drink from one set time to the other, a real four-and-twenty-hours.

And no doctors sit beside him and hold his pulse, whispering, "Hush! Be quiet!"

Well, let us hear the tale!

Chayyim Chaikin is a very poor man, encumbered with

many children, and they, the children, support him.

They are mostly girls, and they work in a factory and make cigarette wrappers, and they earn, some one gulden, others half a gulden, a day, and that not every day. How about Sabbaths and festivals and "shtreik" days? One should thank God for everything, even in their out-of-the-way little town strikes are all the fashion!

And out of that they have to pay rent—for a damp corner in a basement.

To buy clothes and shoes for the lot of them! They have a dress each, but they are two to every pair of shoes.

And then food—such as it is! A bit of bread smeared with an onion, sometimes groats, occasionally there is a bit of taran that burns your heart out, so that after eating it for supper, you can drink a whole night.

When it comes to eating, the bread has to be portioned out like cake.

"Oi, dos Essen, dos Essen seiers!"

Thus Chaike, Chayyim Chaikin's wife, a poor, sick creature, who coughs all night long.

"No evil eye," says the father, and he looks at his children devouring whole slices of bread, and would dearly like to take a mouthful himself, only, if he does so, the two little ones, Fradke and Beilke, will go supperless.

And he cuts his portion of bread in two, and gives it to the little ones, Fradke and Beilke.

Fradke and Beilke stretch out their little thin, black hands, look into their father's eyes, and don't believe him: perhaps he is joking? Children are nashers, they play with father's piece of bread, till at last they begin taking bites out of it. The mother sees and exclaims, coughing all the while:

"It is nothing but eating and stuffing!"

The father cannot bear to hear it, and is about to answer her, but he keeps silent—he can't say anything, it is not for him to speak! Who is he in the house? A broken potsherd, the last and least, no good to anyone, no good to them, no good to himself.

Because the fact is he does nothing, absolutely nothing; not because he won't do anything, or because it doesn't befit him, but because there is nothing to do—and there's an end of it! The whole townlet complains of there being nothing to do! It is just a crowd of Jews driven together. Delightful! They're packed like herrings in a barrel, they squeeze each other close, all for love.

"Well-a-day!" thinks Chaikin, "it's something to have children; other people haven't even that. But to depend on one's children is quite another thing and not a happy one!" Not that they grudge him his keep—Heaven forbid! But he cannot take it from them, he really cannot!

He knows how hard they work, he knows how the strength is wrung out of them to the last drop; he knows it well!

Every morsel of bread is a bit of their health and strength—he drinks his children's blood! No, the thought is too dreadful!

"Tatinke, why don't you eat?" ask the children.

"Today is a fast day with me," answers Chayyim Chaikin.

"Another fast? How many fasts have you?" "Not so many as there are days in the week."

And Chayyim Chaikin speaks the truth when he says that he has many fasts, and yet there are days on which he eats.

But he likes the days on which he fasts better.

First, they are pleasing to God, and it means a little bit more of the world-to-come, the interest grows, and the capital grows with it.

"Secondly" (he thinks), "no money is wasted on me. Of course, I am accountable to no one, and nobody ever questions me as to how I spend it, but what do I want money for, when I can get along without it?

"And what is the good of feeling one's self a little higher than a beast? A beast eats every day, but I can go without food for one or two days. A man *should* be above a beast!

"O, if a man could only raise himself to a level where he could live without eating at all! But there are one's confounded insides!" So thinks Chayyim Chaikin, for hunger has made a philosopher of him.

"The insides, the necessity of eating, these are the causes of the world's evil! The insides and the necessity of eating have made a pauper of me, and drive my children to toil in the sweat of their brow and risk their lives for a bit of bread!

"Suppose a man had no need to eat! Ai—ai—ai! My children would all stay at home! An end to toil, an end to moil, an end to 'shtreikeven,' an end to the risking of life, an end to factory and factory owners, to rich men and paupers, an end to jealousy and hatred and fighting and shedding of blood! All gone and done with! Gone and done with! A paradise! a paradise!"

So reasons Chayyim Chaikin, and, lost in speculation, he pities the world, and is grieved to the heart to think that God should have made man so little above the beast.

The day on which Chayyim Chaikin fasts is, as I told you, his best day, and a *real* fast day, like the Ninth of Ab, for instance—he is ashamed to confess it—is a festival for him!

You see, it means not to eat, not to be a beast, not to be guilty of the children's blood, to earn the reward of a Mitzveh, and to weep to heart's content on the ruins of the Temple.

For how can one weep when one is full? How can a full man grieve? Only he can grieve whose soul is faint within him! The good year knows how some folk answer it to their conscience, giving in to their insides—afraid of fasting! Buy them a groschen worth of oats, for charity's sake!

Thus would Chayyim Chaikin scorn those who bought themselves off the fast, and dropped a hard coin into the collecting box.

The Ninth of Ab is the hardest fast of all—so the world has it.

Chayyim Chaikin cannot see why. The day is long, is it? Then the night is all the shorter. It's hot out of doors, is it? Who asks you to go loitering about in the sun? Sit in the Shool and recite the prayers, of which, thank God, there are plenty.

"I tell you," persists Chayyim Chaikin, "that the Ninth of Ab is the easiest of the fasts, because it is the best, the very best!

"For instance, take the Day of Atonement fast! It is written, 'And you shall mortify your bodies.' What for? To get a clean bill and a good year.

"It doesn't say that you are to fast on the Ninth of Ab, but you fast of your own accord, because how could you

31

eat on the day when the Temple was wrecked, and Jews were killed, women ripped up, and children dashed to pieces?

"It doesn't say that you are to weep on the Ninth of Ab, but you *do* weep. How could anyone restrain his tears when he thinks of what we lost that day?"

"The pity is, there should be only one Ninth of Ab!" says Chayyim Chaikin.

"Well, and the Seventeenth of Tammuz!" suggests someone.

"And there is only one Seventeenth of Tammuz!" answers Chayyim Chaikin, with a sigh.

"Well, and the Fast of Gedaliah? and the Fast of Esther?" continues the same person.

"Only one of each!" and Chayyim Chaikin sighs again.

"Reb Chayyim, you are greedy for fasts, are you?"

"More fasts, more fasts!" says Chayyim Chaikin, and he takes upon himself to fast on the eve of the Ninth of Ab as well, two days at a stretch.

What do you think of fasting two days in succession? Isn't that a treat? It is hard enough to have to break one's fast after the Ninth of Ab, without eating on the eve thereof as well.

One forgets that one *has* insides, that such a thing exists as the necessity to eat, and one is free of the habit that drags one down to the level of the beast.

The difficulty lies in the drinking! I mean, in the not drinking. "If I" (thinks Chayyim Chaikin) "allowed myself one glass of water a day, I could fast a whole week till Sabbath."

You think I say that for fun? Not at all! Chayyim Chaikin is a man of his word. When he says a thing, it's said and done! The whole week preceding the Ninth of Ab he ate nothing, he lived on water.

Who should notice? His wife, poor thing, is sick, the elder children are out all day in the factory, and the younger ones do not understand. Fradke and Beilke only know when they are hungry (and they are always hungry), the heart yearns within them, and they want to eat.

"Today you shall have an extra piece of bread," says the father, and cuts his own in two, and Fradke and Beilke stretch out their dirty little hands for it, and are overjoyed.

"Tatinke, you are not eating," remark the elder girls at supper, "this is not a fast day!"

"And no more *do* I fast!" replies the father, and thinks: "That was a take-in, but not a lie, because, after all, a glass of water—that is not eating and not fasting, either."

When it comes to the eve of the Ninth of Ab, Chayyim feels so light and airy as he never felt before, not because it is time to prepare for the fast by taking a meal, not because he may eat. On the contrary, he feels that if he took anything solid into his mouth, it would not go down, but stick in his throat.

That is, his heart is very sick, and his hands and feet shake; his body is attracted earthwards, his strength fails, he feels like fainting. But fie, what an idea! To fast a whole week, to arrive at the eve of the Ninth of Ab, and not hold out to the end! Never!

And Chayyim Chaikin takes his portion of bread and potato, calls Fradke and Beilke, and whispers:

"Children, take this and eat it, but don't let Mother see!"

And Fradke and Beilke take their father's share of food, and look wonderingly at his livid face and shaking hands.

Chayyim sees the children snatch at the bread and munch and swallow, and he shuts his eyes, and rises from his place. He cannot wait for the other girls to come home from the factory, but takes his book of Lamentations, puts off his shoes, and drags himself—it is all he can do—to the Shool.

He is nearly the first to arrive. He secures a seat next the reader, on an overturned bench, lying with its feet in the air, and provides himself with a bit of burned-down candles, which he glues with its drippings to the foot of the bench, leans against the corner of the platform, opens his book, "Lament for Zion and all the other towns," and he closes his eyes and sees Zion robed in black, with a black veil over her face, lamenting and weeping and wringing her hands, mourning for her children who fall daily, daily, in foreign lands, for other men's sins.

"And wilt not thou, O Zion, ask of me
Some tidings of the children from thee reft?
I bring thee greetings over land and sea,
From those remaining—from the remnant left!—"

And he opens his eyes and sees:

A bright sunbeam has darted in through the dull, dusty windowpane, a beam of the sun which is setting yonder behind the town. And though he shuts them again, he still sees the beam, and not only the beam, but the whole sun, the bright, beautiful sun, and no one can see it but him! Chayyim Chaikin looks at the sun and sees it—and that's all! How is it? It must be because he has done with the world and its necessities—he feels happy—he feels light—

he can bear anything—he will have an easy fast—do you know, he will have an easy fast, an easy fast!

Chayyim Chaikin shuts his eyes, and sees a strange world, a new world, such as he never saw before. Angels seem to hover before his eyes, and he looks at them, and recognizes his children in them, all his children, big and little, and he wants to say something to them, and cannot speak—he wants to explain to them, that he cannot help it—it is not his fault! How should it, no evil eye! be his fault, that so many Jews are gathered together in one place and squeeze each other, all for love, squeeze each other to death for love? How can he help it, if people desire other people's sweat, other people's blood? if people have not learned to see that one should not drive a man as a horse is driven to work? that a horse is also to be pitied, one of God's creatures, a living thing?

And Chayyim Chaikin keeps his eyes shut, and sees, sees everything. And everything is bright and light, and curls like smoke, and he feels something is going out of him, from inside, from his heart, and is drawn upward and loses itself from the body, and he feels very light, very, very light, and he gives a sigh—a long, deep sigh—and feels still lighter, and after that he feels nothing at all—absolutely nothing at all—Yes, he has an easy fast.

When Bäre the beadle, a red-haired Jew with thick lips, came into the Shool in his socks with the worn-down heels, and saw Chayyim Chaikin leaning with his head back, and his eyes open, he was angry, thought Chayyim was dozing, and he began to grumble:

"He ought to be ashamed of himself—reclining like that—came here for a nap, did he?—Reb Chayyim, excuse me, Reb Chayyim!—"

But Chayyim Chaikin did not hear him.

The last rays of the sun streamed in through the Shool window, right onto Chayyim Chaikin's quiet face with the black, shining, curly hair, the black, bushy brows, the half-open, black, kindly eyes, and lit the dead, pale, still, hungry face through and through.

I told you how it would be: Chayyim Chaikin had an easy fast!

THE PASSOVER GUEST

"I have a Passover guest for you, Reb Yoneh, such a guest as you never had since you became a householder."

"What sort is he?"

"A real Oriental citron!"

"What does that mean?"

"It means a 'silken Jew,' a personage of distinction. The only thing against him is—he doesn't speak our language."

"What does he speak, then?"

"Hebrew."

"Is he from Jerusalem?"

"I don't know where he comes from, but his words are full of *a*'s."

Such was the conversation that took place between my father and the beadle, a day before Passover, and I was wild with curiosity to see the "guest" who didn't understand Yiddish, and who talked with *a*'s. I had already noticed, in synagogue, a strange-looking individual, in a fur cap, and a Turkish robe striped blue, red, and yellow. We boys crowded round him on all sides, and stared, and then caught it hot from the beadle, who said children had no business "to creep into a stranger's face" like that. Prayers over, everyone greeted the stranger, and wished him a happy Passover, and he, with a sweet smile on his red cheeks set in a round grey beard, replied to each one, "Shalom! Shalom!" instead of our Sholom. This "Shalom! Shalom!" of his sent us boys into fits of laughter. The beadle grew very angry, and pursued us with slaps. We eluded him, and stole deviously back to the stranger, listened to his "Shalom! Shalom!" exploded with laughter, and escaped anew from the hands of the beadle.

I am puffed up with pride as I follow my father and his guest to our house, and feel how all my comrades envy me. They stand looking after us, and every now and then I turn my head, and put out my tongue at them. The walk home is silent. When we arrive, my father greets my mother with "a happy Passover!" and the guest nods his head so that his fur cap shakes. "Shalom! Shalom!" he says. I think of my comrades, and hide my head under the table, not to burst out laughing. But I shoot continual glances at the guest, and his appearance pleases me; I like his Turkish robe, striped yellow, red, and blue, his fresh, red cheeks set in a curly grey beard, his beautiful black eyes that look out so pleasantly from beneath his bushy eyebrows. And I see that my father is pleased with him, too, that he is delighted with him. My mother looks at him as though he were something more than a man, and no one speaks to him but my father, who offers him the cushioned reclining-seat at table.

Mother is taken up with the preparations for the Passover meal, and Rikel the maid is helping her. It is only when the time comes for saying Kiddush that my father and the guest hold a Hebrew conversation. I am proud to find that I understand nearly every word of it. Here it is in full.

My father: "Nu?" (That means, "Won't you please say Kiddush?")

The guest: "Nu-nu!" (meaning, "Say it rather yourself!")

My father: "Nu-O?" ("Why not you?")

The guest: "O-nu?" ("Why should I?")

My father: "I-O!" ("You first!")

The guest: "O-ai!" ("You first!")

My father: "Ê-o-i!" ("I beg of you to say it!")

The guest: "Ai-o-ê!" ("I beg of you!")

My father: "Ai-e-o-nu?" ("Why should you refuse?")

The guest: "Oi-o-e-nu-nu!" ("If you insist, then I must.")

And the guest took the cup of wine from my father's hand, and recited a Kiddush. But what a Kiddush! A Kiddush such as we had never heard before, and shall never hear again. First, the Hebrew—all *a*'s. Secondly, the voice, which seemed to come, not out of his beard, but out of the striped Turkish robe. I thought of my comrades, how they would have laughed, what slaps would have rained down, had they been present at that Kiddush.

Being alone, I was able to contain myself. I asked my father the Four Questions, and we all recited the Haggadah together. And I was elated to think that such a guest was ours, and no one else's.

Our sage who wrote that one should not talk at meals (may he forgive me for saying so!) did not know Jewish life. When shall a Jew find time to talk, if not during a meal? Especially at *Passover*, when there is so much to say before the meal and after it. Rikel the maid handed the water, we washed our hands, repeated the Benediction, mother helped us to fish, and my father turned up his sleeves, and started a long Hebrew talk with the guest. He began with the first question one Jew asks another:

"What is your name?"

To which the guest replied all in *a*'s and all in one breath:

"Ayak Bakar Gashal Damas Hanoch Vassam Za'an Chafaf Tatzatz."

My father remained with his fork in the air, staring in amazement at the possessor of so long a name. I coughed and looked under the table, and my mother said, "Favele, you should be careful eating fish, or you might be choked with a bone," while she gazed at our guest with awe. She appeared overcome by his name, although unable to understand it. My father, who understood, thought it necessary to explain it to her.

"You see, Ayak Bakar, that is our Alef-Bes inverted. It is apparently their custom to name people after the alphabet."

"Alef-Bes! Alef-Bes!" repeated the guest with the sweet smile on his red cheeks, and his beautiful black eyes rested on us all, including Rikel the maid, in the most friendly fashion.

Having learnt his name, my father was anxious to know whence, from what land, he came. I understood this from the names of countries and towns which I caught, and from what my father translated for my mother, giving her a Yiddish version of nearly every phrase. And my mother was quite overcome by every single thing she heard, and Rikel the maid was overcome likewise. And no wonder! It is not every day that a person comes from perhaps two thousand miles away, from a land only to be reached across seven seas and a desert, the desert journey alone requiring forty days and nights. And when you get near to the land, you have to climb a mountain of which the top reaches into the clouds, and this is covered with ice, and dreadful winds blow there, so that there is peril of death! But once the mountain is safely climbed, and the land is reached, one beholds a terrestrial Eden. Spices, cloves, herbs, and every kind of fruit—apples, pears, and oranges, grapes, dates, and olives, nuts and quantities of figs. And the houses there are all built of deal, and roofed with silver, the furniture is gold (here the guest cast a look at our silver cups, spoons, forks, and knives), and brilliants, pearls, and diamonds bestrew the roads, and no one cares to take the trouble of picking them up, they are of no value there. (He was looking at my mother's diamond earrings, and at the pearls round her white neck.)

"You hear that?" my father asked her, with a happy face.

"I hear," she answered, and added: "Why don't they bring some over here? They could make money by it. Ask him that, Yoneh!"

My father did so, and translated the answer for my mother's benefit:

"You see, when you arrive there, you may take what you like, but when you leave the country, you must leave everything in it behind, too, and if they shake out of you no matter what, you are done for."

"What do you mean?" questioned my mother,

terrified.

"I mean, they either hang you on a tree, or they stone you with stones."

The more tales our guest told us, the more thrilling they became, and just as we were finishing the dumplings and taking another sip or two of wine, my father inquired to whom the country belonged. Was there a king there? And he was soon translating, with great delight, the following reply:

"The country belongs to the Jews who live there, and who are called Sefardîm. And they have a king, also a Jew, and a very pious one, who wears a fur cap, and who is called Joseph ben Joseph. He is the high priest of the Sefardîm, and drives out in a gilded carriage, drawn by six fiery horses. And when he enters the synagogue, the Levites meet him with songs."

"There are Levites who sing in your synagogue?" asked my father, wondering, and the answer caused his face to shine with joy.

"What do you think?" he said to my mother. "Our guest tells me that in his country there is a temple, with priests and Levites and an organ."

"Well, and an altar?" questioned my mother, and my father told her:

"He says they have an altar, and sacrifices, he says, and golden vessels—everything just as we used to have it in Jerusalem."

And with these words my father sighs deeply, and my mother, as she looks at him, sighs also, and I cannot understand the reason. Surely we should be proud and glad to think we have such a land, ruled over by a Jewish king and high priest, a land with Levites and an organ, with an altar and sacrifices—and bright, sweet thoughts enfold me, and carry me away as on wings to that happy Jewish land where the houses are of pine-wood and roofed with silver, where the furniture is gold, and diamonds and pearls lie scattered in the street. And I feel sure, were I really there, I should know what to do—I should know how to hide things—they would shake nothing out of *me*. I should certainly bring home a lovely present for my mother, diamond earrings and several pearl necklaces. I look at the one mother is wearing, at her earrings, and I feel a great desire to be in that country. And it occurs to me, that after Passover I will travel there with our guest, secretly, no one shall know. I will only speak of it to our guest, open my heart to him, tell him the whole truth, and beg him to take me there, if only for a little while. He will certainly do so, he is a very kind and approachable person, he looks at everyone, even at Rikel the maid, in such a friendly, such a very friendly way!

"So I think, and it seems to me, as I watch our guest, that he has read my thoughts, and that his beautiful black eyes say to me:

"Keep it dark, little friend, wait till after Passover, then we shall manage it!"

I dreamt all night long. I dreamt of a desert, a temple, a high priest, and a tall mountain. I climb the mountain. Diamonds and pearls grow on the trees, and my comrades sit on the boughs, and shake the jewels down onto the ground, whole showers of them, and I stand and gather them, and stuff them into my pockets, and, strange to say, however many I stuff in, there is still room! I stuff and stuff, and still there is room! I put my hand into my pocket, and draw out—not pearls and brilliants, but fruits of all kinds—apples, pears, oranges, olives, dates, nuts, and figs. This makes me very unhappy, and I toss from side to side. Then I dream of the temple, I hear the priests chant, and the Levites sing, and the organ play. I want to go inside and I cannot—Rikel the maid has hold of me, and will not let me go. I beg of her and scream and cry, and again I am very unhappy, and toss from side to side. I wake—and see my father and mother standing there, half dressed, both pale, my father hanging his head, and my mother wringing her hands, and with her soft eyes full of tears. I feel at once that something has gone very wrong, very wrong indeed, but my childish head is incapable of imagining the greatness of the disaster.

The fact is this: our guest from beyond the desert and the seven seas has disappeared, and a lot of things have disappeared with him: all the silver wine-cups, all the silver spoons, knives, and forks; all my mother's ornaments, all the money that happened to be in the house, and also Rikel the maid!

A pang goes through my heart. Not on account of the silver cups, the silver spoons, knives, and forks that have vanished; not on account of mother's ornaments or of the money, still less on account of Rikel the maid, a good riddance! But because of the happy, happy land whose roads were strewn with brilliants, pearls, and diamonds; because of the temple with the priests, the Levites, and the organ; because of the altar and the sacrifices; because of all the other beautiful things that have been taken from me, taken, taken, taken!

I turn my face to the wall, and cry quietly to myself.

GYMNASIYE

A man's worst enemy, I tell you, will never do him the harm he does himself, especially when a woman interferes; that is, a wife. Whom do you think I have in mind when I say that? My own self! Look at me and think. What would you take me for? Just an ordinary Jew. It doesn't say on my nose whether I have money, or not, or whether I am very low indeed, does it?

It may be that I once *had* money, and not only that—money in itself is nothing—but I can tell you, I earned a living, and that respectably and quietly, without worry and flurry, not like some people who like to live in a whirl.

No, my motto is, "More haste, less speed."

I traded quietly, went bankrupt a time or two quietly, and quietly went to work again. But there is a God in the world, and He blessed me with a wife—as she isn't here, we can speak openly—a wife like any other, that is, at first glance she isn't so bad—not at all! In person (no evil eye!) twice my height; not an ugly woman, quite a beauty, you may say; an intelligent woman, quite a man—and that's the whole trouble! Oi, it isn't good when the wife is a man! The Almighty knew what He was about when, at the creation, he formed Adam first and then Eve. But what's the use of telling her that, when *she* says, "If the Almighty created Adam first and then Eve, that's *His* affair, but if he put more sense into my heel than into your head, no more am I to blame for that!"

"What is all this about?" say I.— "It's about that which should be first and foremost with you," says she. "But I have to be the one to think of everything—even about sending the boy to the Gymnasiye [a school that prepares pupils for university entrance]!"— "Where," say I, "is it 'written' that my boy should go to the Gymnasiye? Can I not afford to have him taught Torah at home?"— "I've told you a hundred and fifty times," says she, "that you won't persuade me to go against the world! And the world," says she, "has decided that children should go to the Gymnasiye."— "In my opinion," say I, "the world is mad!"—"And you," says she, "are the only sane person in it? A pretty thing it would be," says she, "if the world were to follow you!"— "Every man," say I, "should decide on his own course."— "If my enemies," says she, "and my friends' enemies, had as little in pocket and bag, in box and chest, as you have in your head, the world would be a different place."— "Woe to the man," say I, "who needs to be advised by his wife!"— "And woe to the wife," says she, "who has that man to her husband!"—Now if you can argue with a woman who, when you say one thing, maintains the contrary, when you give her one word, treats you to a dozen, and who, if you bid her shut up, cries, or even, I beg of you, faints—well, I envy you, that's all! In short, up and down, this way and that way, she got the best of it—she, not I, because the fact is, when she wants a thing, it has to be!

Well, what next? Gymnasiye! The first thing was to prepare the boy for the elementary class in the Junior Preparatory. I must say, I did not see anything very alarming in that. It seemed to me that anyone of our Cheder boys, an Alef-Bes scholar, could tuck it all into his belt, especially a boy like mine, for whose equal you might search an empire, and not find him. I am a father, not of you be it said! but that boy has a memory that beats everything! To cut a long story short, he went up for examination and—did not pass! You ask the reason? He only got a two in arithmetic; they said he was weak at calculation, in the science of mathematics. What do you think of that? He has a memory that beats everything! I tell you, you might search an empire for his like—and they come talking to me about mathematics! Well, he failed to pass, and it vexed me very much. If he *was* to go up for examination, let him succeed. However, being a man and not a woman, I made up my mind to it—it's a misfortune, but a Jew is used to that. Only what was the use of talking to her with that bee in her bonnet? Once for all, Gymnasiye! I reason with her. "Tell me," say I, "(may you be well!) what is the good of it? He's safe," say I, "from military service, being an only son, and as for Parnosseh, devil I need it for Parnosseh! What do I care if he *does* become a trader like his father, a merchant like the rest of the Jews? If he is destined to become a rich man, a banker, I don't see that I'm to be pitied."

Thus do I reason with her as with the wall. "So much the better," says she, "if he has not been entered for the Junior Preparatory."—"What now?" say I.

"Now," says she, "he can go direct to the Senior Preparatory."

Well, Senior Preparatory, there's nothing so terrible in that, for the boy has a head, I tell you! You might search an empire.... And what was the result? Well, what do you suppose? Another two instead of a five, not in mathematics this time—a fresh calamity! His spelling is not what it should be. That is, he can spell all right, but he gets a bit mixed with the two Russian *e*'s. That is, he puts them in right enough, why shouldn't he? only not in their proper places. Well, there's a misfortune for you! I guess I won't find the way to Poltava fair if the child cannot put the *e*'s where they belong! When they brought the good news, *she* turned the town inside out; ran to the director, declared that the boy *could* do it; to prove it, let him be had up again! They paid her as much attention as if she were last year's snow, put a two, and another sort of two, and a two with a dash! Call me nutcrackers, but there was a commotion. "Failed again!" say I to her. "And if so," say I, "what is to be done? Are we to commit suicide? A Jew," say I, "is used to that sort of thing," upon which she fired up and blazed away and stormed and scolded as only she can. But I let you off! He, poor child, was in a pitiable state. Talk of cruelty to animals! Just think: the other boys in little white buttons, and not he! I reason with him: "You little fool! What does it matter? Who ever heard of an examination at which everyone passed? Somebody must stay at home, mustn't they? Then why not you? There's really nothing to make such a fuss about." My wife, overhearing, goes off into a fresh fury, and falls upon me. "A fine comforter *you* are," says she, "who asked you to console him with that sort of nonsense? You'd better see about getting him a proper teacher," says she, "a private teacher, a Russian, for grammar!"

You hear that? Now I must have two teachers for him—one teacher and a Rebbe are not enough. Up and down, this way and that way, she got the best of it, as usual.

What next? We engaged a second teacher, a Russian this time, not a Jew, preserve us, but a real Gentile, because grammar in the first class, let me tell you, is no trifle, no shredded horseradish! Gra-ma-ti-ke, indeed! The two *e*'s! Well, I was telling about the teacher that God sent us for our sins. It's enough to make one blush to remember the way he treated us, as though we had been the mud under his feet. Laughed at us to our face, he did, devil take him, and the one and only thing he could teach him was: tshasnok, tshasnoka, tshasnoku, tshasnokom. If it hadn't been for *her*, I should have had him by the throat, and out into the street with his blessed grammar. But to *her* it was all right and as it should be. Now the boy will know which *e* to put. If you'll believe me, they tormented him through that whole winter, for he was not to be had up for slaughter till about Pentecost. Pentecost over, he went up for examination, and this time he brought home no more two's, but a four and a five. There was great joy—we congratulate! we congratulate! Wait a bit, don't be in such a hurry with your congratulations! We don't know yet for certain whether he has got in or not. We shall not know till August. Why not till August? Why not before? Go and ask *them*. What is to be done? A Jew is used to that sort of thing.

August—and I gave a glance out of the corner of my eye. She was up and doing! From the director to the inspector, from the inspector to the director! "Why are you running from Shmunin to Bunin," say I, "like a poisoned mouse?"

"You asking why?" says she. "Aren't you a native of this place? You don't seem to know how it is nowadays with the Gymnasiyes and the percentages?" And what came of it? He did *not* pass! You ask why? Because he hadn't two fives. If he had had two fives, then, they say, perhaps he would have got in. You hear—perhaps! How do you like that *perhaps?* Well, I'll let you off what I had to bear from her. As for him, the little boy, it was pitiful. Lay with his face in the cushion, and never stopped crying till we promised him another teacher. And we got him a student from the Gymnasiye itself, to prepare him for the second class, but after quite another fashion, because the second class is no joke. In the second, besides mathematics and grammar, they require geography, penmanship, and I couldn't for the life of me say what else. I should have thought a bit of the Maharsho was a more difficult thing than all their studies put together, and very likely had more sense in it, too. But what would you have? A Jew learns to put up with things.

In fine, there commenced a series of "lessons," of ouròkki. We rose early—the ouròkki! Prayers and breakfast over—the ouròkki. A whole day—ouròkki. One heard him late at night drumming it over and over: Nominative—dative—instrumental—vocative! It grated so on my ears! I could hardly bear it. Eat? Sleep? Not he! Taking a poor creature and tormenting it like that, all for nothing, I call it cruelty to animals! "The child," say I, "will be ill!" "Bite off your tongue," says she. I was nowhere, and he went up a second time to the slaughter, and brought home nothing but fives! And why not? I tell you, he has a head—there isn't his like! And such a boy for study as never was, always at it, day and night, and repeating to himself between whiles! That's all right then, is it? Was it all right? When it came to the point, and they hung out the names of all the children who were really entered, we looked—mine wasn't there! Then" there was a screaming and a commotion. What a shame! And nothing but fives! *Now* look at her, now see her go, see her run, see her do this and that! In short, she went and she ran and she did this and that and the other—until at last they begged her not to worry them any longer, that is, to tell you the truth, between ourselves, they turned her out, yes! And after they had turned her out, then it was she burst into the house, and showed for the first time, as it were, what she was worth. "Pray," said she, "what sort of a father are you? If you were a good father, an affectionate father, like other fathers, you would have found favor with the director, patronage, recommendations, this—that!" Like a woman, wasn't it? It's not enough, apparently, for me to have my head full of terms and seasons and fairs and notes and bills of exchange and "protests" and all the rest of it. "Do you want me," say I, "to take over your Gymnasiye and your classes, things I'm sick of already?" Do you suppose she listened to what I said? She? Listen? She just kept at it, she sawed and filed and gnawed away like a worm, day and night, day and night! "If your wife," says she, *"were* a wife, and your child, a child—if I were only of so much account in this house!"—"Well," say I, "what would happen?"—"You would lie," says she, "nine ells deep in the earth. I," says she, "would bury you three times a day, so that you should never rise again!"

How do you like that? Kind, wasn't it? That (how goes the saying?) was pouring a pailful of water over a husband for the sake of peace. Of course, you'll understand that I was not silent, either, because, after all, I'm no more than a man, and every man has his feelings. I assure you, you needn't envy me, and in the end she carried the day, as usual.

Well, what next? I began currying favor, getting up an acquaintance, trying this and that; I had to lower myself in people's eyes and swallow slights, for everyone asked questions, and they had every right to do so. "You, no evil eye, Reb Aaron," say they, "are a householder, and inherited a little something from your father. What good year is taking you about to places where a Jew had better not be seen?" Was I to go and tell them I had a wife (may she live one hundred and twenty years!) with this on the brain: Gymnasiye, Gymnasiye, and Gym-na-si-ye? I (much good may it do you!) am, as you see me, no more unlucky than most people, and with God's help I made my way, and got where I wanted, right up to the nobleman, into his cabinet, yes! And sat down with him there to talk it over. I thank Heaven, I can talk to any nobleman, I don't need to have my tongue loosened for me. "What can I do for you?" he asks, and bids me be seated. Say I, and whisper into his ear, "My lord," says I, "we," say I, "are not rich people, but we have," say I, "a boy, and he wishes to study, and I," say I, "wish it, too, but my wife wishes it *very much!*" Says he to me again, "What is it you want?" Say I to him, and edge a bit closer, "My dear lord," say I, "we," say I, "are not rich people, but we have," say I, "a small fortune, and one remarkably clever boy, who," say I, "wishes to study; and I," say I, "also wish it, but my wife wishes it very much!" and I squeeze that "very much" so that he may understand. But he's a Gentile and slow-witted, and he doesn't twig, and this time he asks angrily, "Then, whatever is it you want?!" I quietly put my hand into my pocket and quietly take it out again, and I say quietly: "Pardon me, we," say I, "are not rich people, but we have a little," say I, "fortune, and one remarkably clever boy, who," say I, "wishes to study; and I," say I, "wish it also, but my wife," say I, "wishes it very much indeed!" and I take and press into his hand and this time, yes! he understood, and went and got a notebook, and asked my name and my son's name, and which class I wanted him entered for.

"Oho, lies the wind that way?" think I to myself, and I give him to understand that I am called Katz, Aaron Katz, and my son, Moisheh, Moshke we call him, and I want to get him into the third class. Says he to me, if I am Katz, and my son is Moisheh, Moshke we call him, and he wants to get into class three, I am to bring him in January, and he will certainly be passed. You hear and understand? Quite another thing! Apparently the horse trots as we shoe him. The worst is having to wait. But what is to be done? When they say, Wait! one waits. A Jew is used to waiting.

January—a fresh commotion, a scampering to and fro. Tomorrow there will be a consultation. The director and the inspector and all the teachers of the Gymnasiye will come together, and it's only after the consultation that we shall know if he is entered or not. The time for action has come, and my wife is anywhere but at home. No hot meals, no samovar, no nothing! She is in the Gymnasiye, that is, not in the Gymnasiye, but at it, walking round and round it in the frost, from first thing in the morning, waiting for them to begin coming away from the consultation. The frost bites, there is a tearing east wind, and she paces round and round the building, and waits. Once a woman, always a woman! It seemed to me, that when people have made a promise, it is surely sacred, especially—you understand? But who would reason with a woman? Well, she waited one hour, she waited two, waited three, waited four; the children were all home long ago, and she waited on. She waited (much good may it do you!) till she got what she was waiting for. A door opens, and out comes one of the teachers. She springs and seizes hold on him. Does he know the result of the consultation? Why, says he, should he not? They have passed altogether twenty-five children, twenty-three Christian and two Jewish. Says she, "Who are they?" Says he, "One a Shefselsohn and one a Katz." At the name Katz, my wife shoots home like an arrow from the bow, and bursts into the room in triumph: "Good news! good news! Passed, passed!" and there are tears in her eyes. Of course, I am pleased, too, but I don't feel called upon to go dancing, being a man and not a woman. "It's evidently not much you care?" says she to me. "What makes you think that?" say I.— "This," says she, "you sit there cold as a stone! If you knew how impatient the child is, you would have taken him long ago to the tailor's, and ordered his little uniform," says she, "and a cap and a satchel," says she, "and made a little banquet for our friends."—"Why a banquet, all of a sudden?" say I. "Is there a Bar-Mitzveh? Is there an engagement?" I say all this quite quietly, for, after all, I am a man, not a woman. She grew so angry that she stopped talking. And when a woman stops talking, it's a thousand times worse than when she scolds, because so long as she is scolding at least you hear the sound of the human voice. Otherwise it's talk to the wall! To put it briefly, she got her way—she, not I—as usual.

There was a banquet; we invited our friends and our good friends, and my boy was dressed up from head to foot in a very smart uniform, with white buttons and a cap with a badge in front, quite the district-governor! And it did one's heart good to see him, poor child! There was new life in him, he was so happy, and he shone, I tell you, like the July sun! The company drank to him, and wished him joy: Might he study in health, and finish the course in health, and go on in health, till he reached the university! "Ett!" say I, "we can do with less. Let him only complete the eight classes at the Gymnasiye," say I, "and, please God, I'll make a bridegroom of him, with God's help." Cries my wife, smiling and fixing me with her eye the while, "Tell him," says she, "that he's wrong! He," says she, "keeps to the old-fashioned cut." "Tell her from me," say I, "that' I'm blest if the old-fashioned cut wasn't better than the new." Says she, "Tell him that he (may he forgive me!) is—" The company burst out laughing. "Oi, Reb Aaron," say they, "you have a wife (no evil eye!) who is a Cossack and not a wife at all!" Meanwhile they emptied their wineglasses, and cleared their plates, and we were what is called "lively." I and my wife were what is called "taken into the boat," the little one in the middle, and we made merry till daylight. That morning early we took him to the Gymnasiye. It was very early, indeed, the door was shut, not a soul to be seen. Standing outside there in the frost, we were glad enough when the door opened, and they let us in. Directly after that the small fry began to arrive with their satchels, and there was a noise and a commotion and a chatter and a laughing and a scampering to and fro—a regular fair! Schoolboys jumped over one another, gave each other punches, pokes, and pinches. As I looked at these young hopefuls with the red cheeks, with the merry, laughing eyes, I called to mind our former narrow, dark, and gloomy Cheder of long ago years, and I saw that after all she was right; she might be a woman, but she had a man's head on her shoulders! And as I reflected thus, there came along an individual in gilt buttons, who turned out to be a teacher, and asked what I wanted. I pointed to my boy, and said I had come to bring him to Cheder; that is, to the Gymnasiye. He asked to which class? I tell him, the third, and he has only just been entered. He asks his name. Say 1, "Katz, Moisheh Katz, that is, Moshke Katz." Says he, "Moshke Katz?" He has no Moshke Katz in the third class. "There is," he says, "a Katz, only not a Moshke Katz, but a Morduch—Morduch Katz." Say I, "What Morduch? Moshke, not Morduch!" "Morduch!" he repeats, and thrusts the paper into my face. I to him, "Moshke." He to me, "Morduch!" In short, Moshke—Morduch, Morduch—Moshke, we hammer away till there comes out a fine tale: that which should have been mine is another's. You see what a kettle of fish? A regular Gentile muddle! They have entered a Katz—yes! But, by mistake, another, not ours. You see how it was: there were two Katz's in our town! What do you say to such luck? I have made a bed, and another will lie in it! No, but you ought to know who the other is, *that* Katz, I mean! A nothing of a nobody, an artisan, a bookbinder or a carpenter, quite a harmless little man, but who ever heard of him? A pauper! And *his* son—yes! And mine—no! Isn't it enough to disgust one, I ask you! And you should have seen that poor boy of mine, when he was told to take the badge off his cap! No bride on her wedding-day need shed more tears than were his! And no matter how I reasoned with him, whether I coaxed or scolded, "You see," I said to her, "what you've done! Didn't I tell you that your Gymnasiye was a slaughterhouse for him? I only trust this may have a good ending, that he won't fall ill."— "Let my enemies," said she, "fall ill, if they like. My child," says she, "must enter the Gymnasiye. If he hasn't got in this time, in a year, please God, he *will*. If he hasn't got in," says she, "*here*, he will get in another town—he must get in! Otherwise," says she, "I shall shut an eye, and the earth shall cover me!" You hear what she said? And who, do you suppose, had his way—she or I? When *she* sets her heart on a thing, can there be any question?

Well, I won't make a long story of it. I hunted up and down with him; we went to the ends of the world, wherever there was a town and a Gymnasiye, thither went we! We went up for examination, and were examined, and we passed and passed high, and did not get in—and why? All because of the percentage! You may believe, I looked upon my own self as crazy those days! "Wretch! what is this? What is this flying that you fly from one town to another? What good is to come of it? And suppose he does get in, what then?" No, say what you will, ambition is a great thing. In the end it took hold of me, too, and the Almighty had compassion, and sent me a Gymnasiye in Poland, a "commercial" one, where they took in one Jew to every Christian. It came to fifty percent. But what then? Any Jew who wished his son to enter must bring his Christian with him, and if he passes, that is, the Christian, and one pays his entrance fee, then there is hope. Instead of one bundle, one has two on one's shoulders, you understand? Besides being worn with anxiety about my own, I had to tremble for the other, because if Esau, which Heaven forbid, fail to pass, it's all over with Jacob. But what I went through before I *got* that Christian, a shoemaker's son, Holiava his name was, is not to be described. And the best of all was this—would you believe that my shoemaker, planted in the earth firmly as Korah, insisted on Bible teaching? There was nothing for it but my son had to sit down beside his, and repeat the Old Testament. How came a son of mine to the Old Testament? Ai, don't ask! He can do everything and understands everything.

With God's help the happy day arrived, and they both passed. Is my story finished? Not quite. When it came to their being entered in the books, to writing out a check, my Christian was not to be found! What has happened? He, the Gentile, doesn't care for his son to be among so many Jews—he won't hear of it! Why should he, seeing that all doors are open to him anyhow, and he can get in where he pleases? Tell him it isn't fair? Much good that would be! "Look here," say I, "how much do you want, Pani Holiava?" Says he, "Nothing!" To cut the tale short— up and down, this way and that way, and friends and people interfering, we had him off to a refreshment place, and ordered a glass, and two, and three, before it all came right! Once he was really in, I cried my eyes out, and thanks be to Him whose Name is blessed, and who has delivered me out of all my troubles! When I got home, a fresh worry! What now? My wife has been reflecting and thinking it over: After all, her only son, the apple of her eye—he would be *there* and we *here!* And if so, what, says she, would life be to her? "Well," say I, "what do you propose doing?"— "What I propose doing?" says she, "Can't you guess? I propose," says she, "to be with him."— "You do?" say I. "And the house? What about the house?"— "The house," says she, "is a house." Anything to object to in that? So she was off to him, and I was left alone at home. And what a home! I leave you to imagine. May such a year be to my enemies! My comfort was gone, the business went to the bad. Everything went to the bad, and we were continually writing letters. I wrote to her, she wrote to me—letters went and letters came. Peace to my beloved wife! Peace to my beloved husband! "For Heaven's sake," I write, "what is to be the end of it? After all, I'm no more than a man! A man without a housemistress!" It was as much use as last year's snow; it was she who had her way, she, and not I, as usual.

To make an end of my story, I worked and worried myself to pieces, made a mull of the whole business, sold out, became a poor man, and carried my bundle over to them. Once there, I took a look round to see where I was in the world, nibbled here and there, just managed to make my way a bit, and entered into a partnership with a trader, quite a respectable man, yes! A well-to-do householder, holding office in the Shool, but at bottom a deceiver, a swindler, a pickpocket, who was nearly the ruin of me! You can imagine what a cheerful state of things it was. Meanwhile I come home one evening, and see my boy come to meet me, looking strangely red in the face, and without a badge on his cap. Say I to him, "Look here, Moshehl, where's your badge?" Says he to me, "Whatever badge?" Say I, "The button." Says he, "Whatever button?" Say I, "The button off your cap." It was a new cap with a new badge, only just bought for the festival! He grows redder than before, and says, "Taken off." Say I, "What do you mean by 'taken off'?" Says he, "I am free." Say I, "What do you mean by 'you are free'?" Says he, "We are *all* free." Say I, "What do you mean by 'we are *all* free'?" Says he, "We are not going back any more." Say I, "What do you mean by 'we are not going back'?" Says he, "We have united in the resolve to stay away." Say I, "What do you mean by '*you*' have united in a resolve? Who are 'you'? What is all this? Bless your grandmother," say I, "do you suppose I have been through all this for you to unite in a resolve? Alas! and alack!" say I, "for you and me and all of us! May it please God not to let this be visited on Jewish heads, because always and everywhere," say I, "Jews are the scapegoats." I speak thus to him and grow angry and reprove him as a father usually does reprove a child. But I have a wife (long life to her!), and she comes running, and washes my head for me, tells me I don't know what is going on in the world, that the world is quite another world to what it used to be, an intelligent world, an open world, a free world, "a world," says she, "in which all are equal, in which there are no rich and no poor, no masters and no servants, no sheep and no shears, no cats, rats, no piggy-wiggy—" "Te-te-te!" say I, "where have you learned such fine language? a new speech," say I, "with new words. Why not open the henhouse, and let out the hens? Chuck—Chuck—Chuck, hurrah for freedom!" Upon which she blazes up as if I had poured ten pails of hot water over her. And now for it! As only *they* can! Well, one must sit it out and listen to the end. The worst of it is, there is no end. "Look here," say I, "hush!" say I, "and now let be!" say I, and beat upon my breast. "I have sinned!" say I, "I have transgressed, and now stop," say I, "if you would only be quiet!" But she won't hear, and she won't see. No, she says, she will know why and wherefore and for goodness' sake and exactly, and just how it was, and what it means, and how it happened, and once more and a second time, and all over again from the beginning!

I beg of you—who set the whole thing going? A—woman!

ABOUT THE AUTHOR

Humoristic Yiddish author Sholem Aleichem, pseudonym of Solomon Rabinowitz, was born in Kiev, Russia, March 2, 1859. He began his career as a writer of short Yiddish stories in the Russian-Yiddish press. Because of the Kishinev pogroms, he came to the United States in 1906, and was received with great acclaim by his coreligionists. He returned later to Russia, where he met with pecuniary reverses, which were at once relieved by his many thousands of warm admirers.

At the beginning of World War I, Mr. Rabinowitz, who was at a health resort near Berlin, was detained and finally sent to Denmark. He returned to the United States in December 1914, where he was again feted and lavishly entertained. In the United States he wrote stories for the Yiddish dailies, many of which have been translated into English. He is best known for his sympathetic, kindly, humorous treatment of Ghetto life. His admirers in the United States have called him "the Yiddish Mark Twain." His works include novels, short stories, plays, and an autobiography. The musical *Fiddler on the Roof* is based on his stories about Tevye the Milkman.

Rabinowitz requested that upon his death his friends not erect any monument to his memory because he preferred his writings to be his only monument. HE died in New York City on May 13, 1916 from tuberculosis and diabetes. He left in his will a provision "for Jewish writers (in Yiddish and in Hebrew)" consisting of five percent of the royalties from his works, up to 5,000 rubles a year.

Made in the USA
San Bernardino, CA
16 January 2016